I Went for a Wa

Story by Shanti Wintergate Illustrated by Gregory

www.hollywoodjersey.com
www.iwentforawalk.com

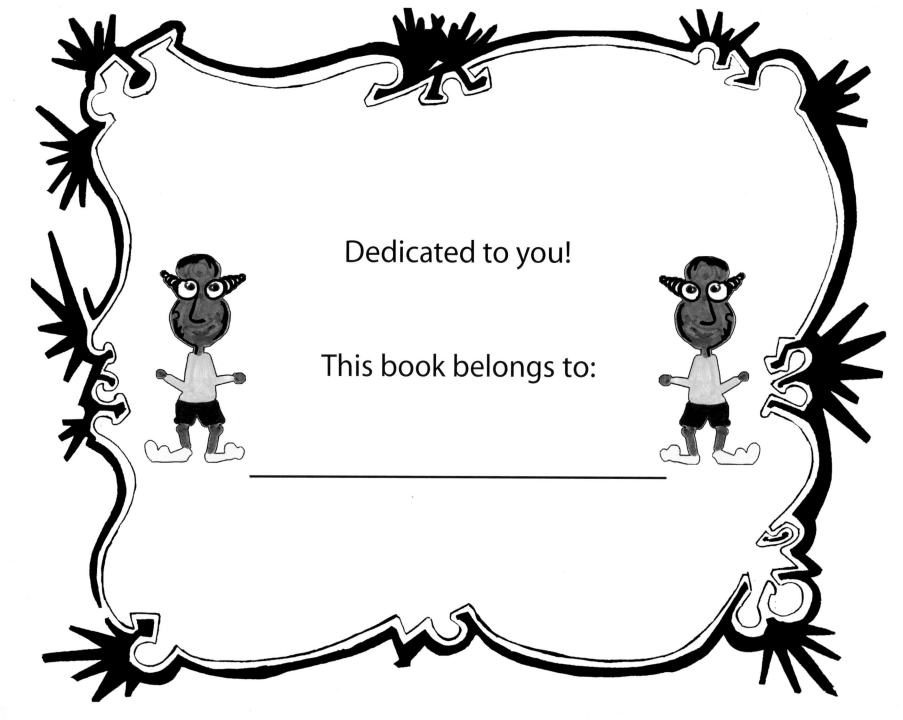

Dedicated to you!

This book belongs to:

_____

Chapters

Chapter One: Earth

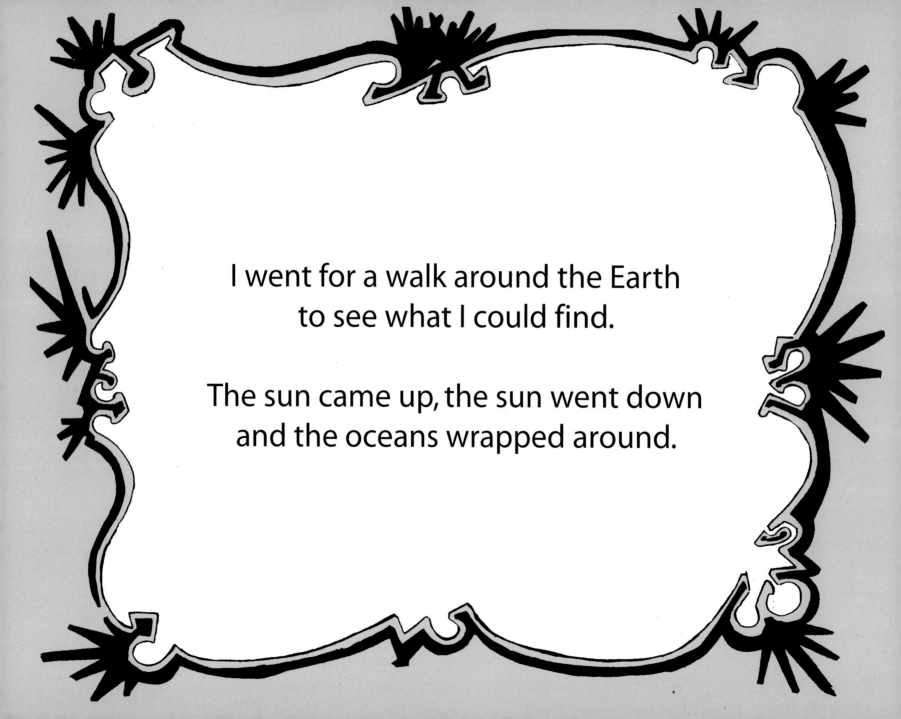

I went for a walk around the Earth
to see what I could find.

The sun came up, the sun went down
and the oceans wrapped around.

I climbed with mountain goats, monkeys and bears.

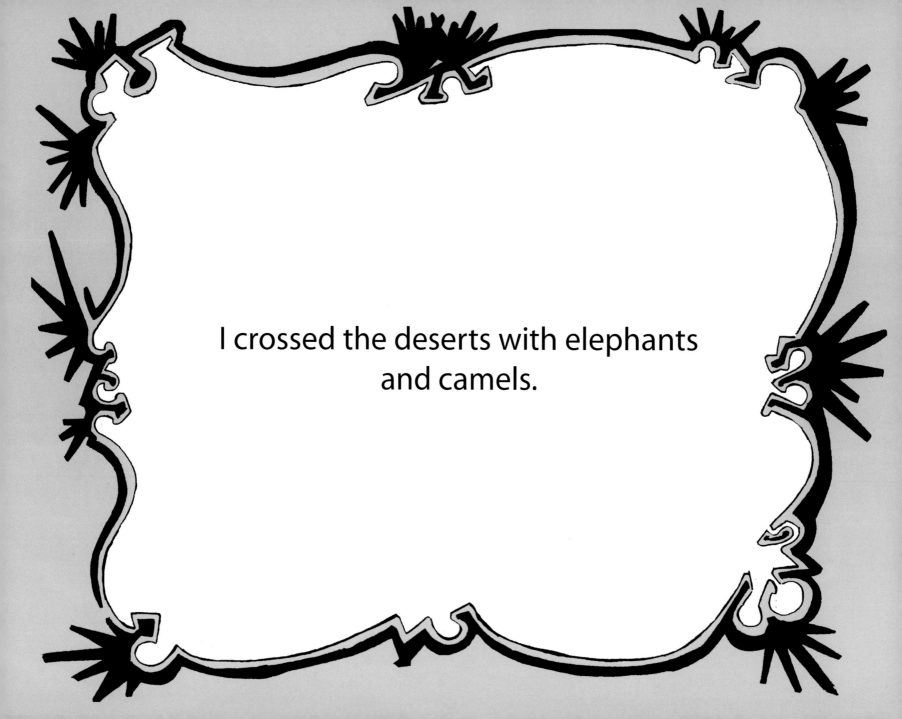

I crossed the deserts with elephants and camels.

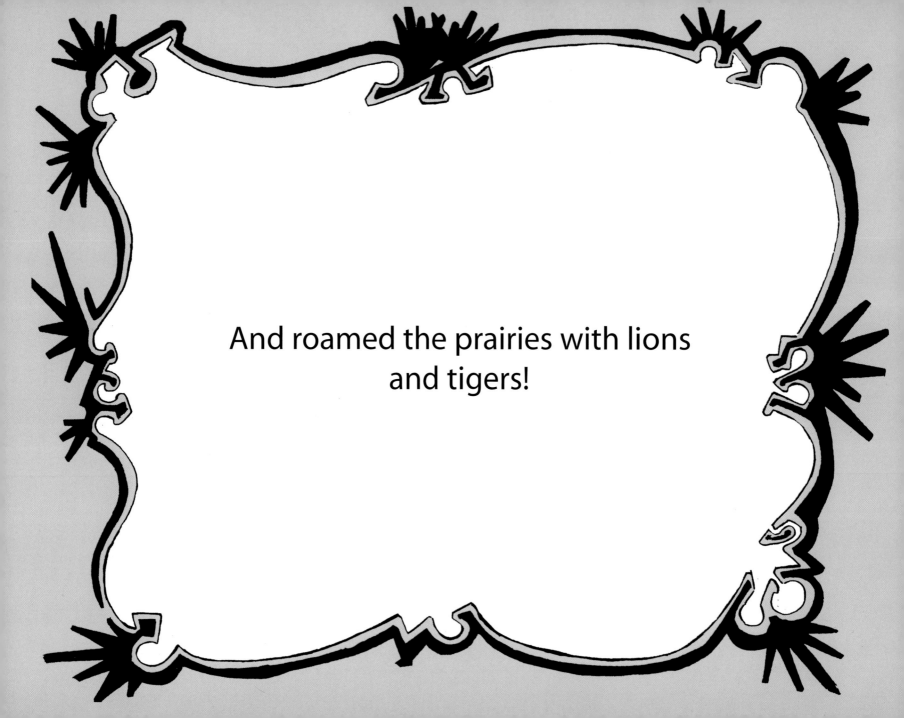

And roamed the prairies with lions and tigers!

Just when I thought I'd gone far enough,
I looked into the sky and began to
float up!

I sat on a star and watched from above.
The Earth that was so BIG
seemed so very small.

I opened the fridge with one swift pull
but to my surprise the fridge
wasn't very full.

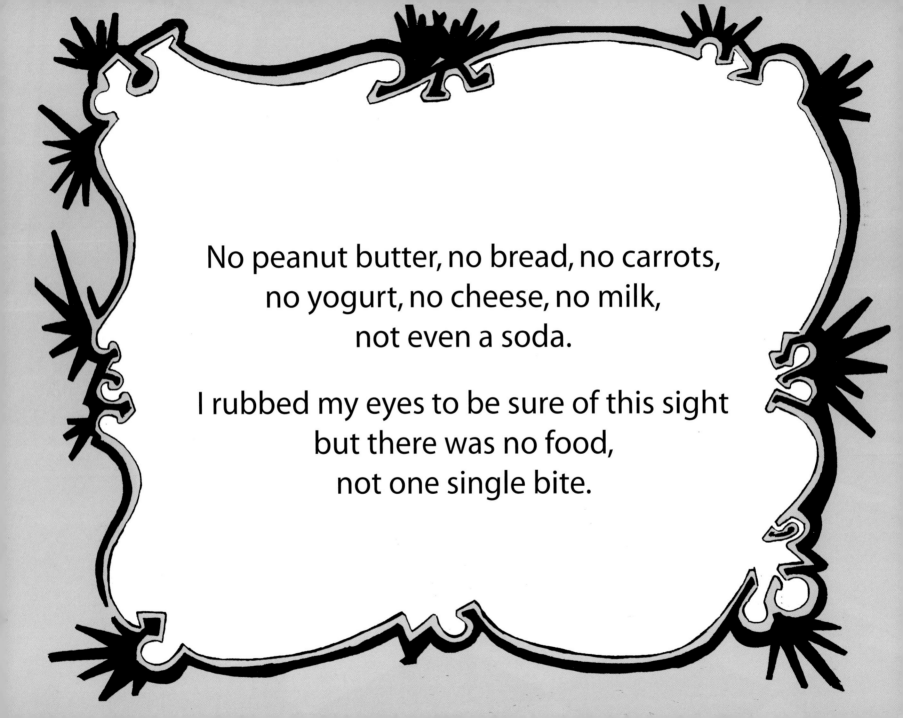

No peanut butter, no bread, no carrots,
no yogurt, no cheese, no milk,
not even a soda.

I rubbed my eyes to be sure of this sight
but there was no food,
not one single bite.

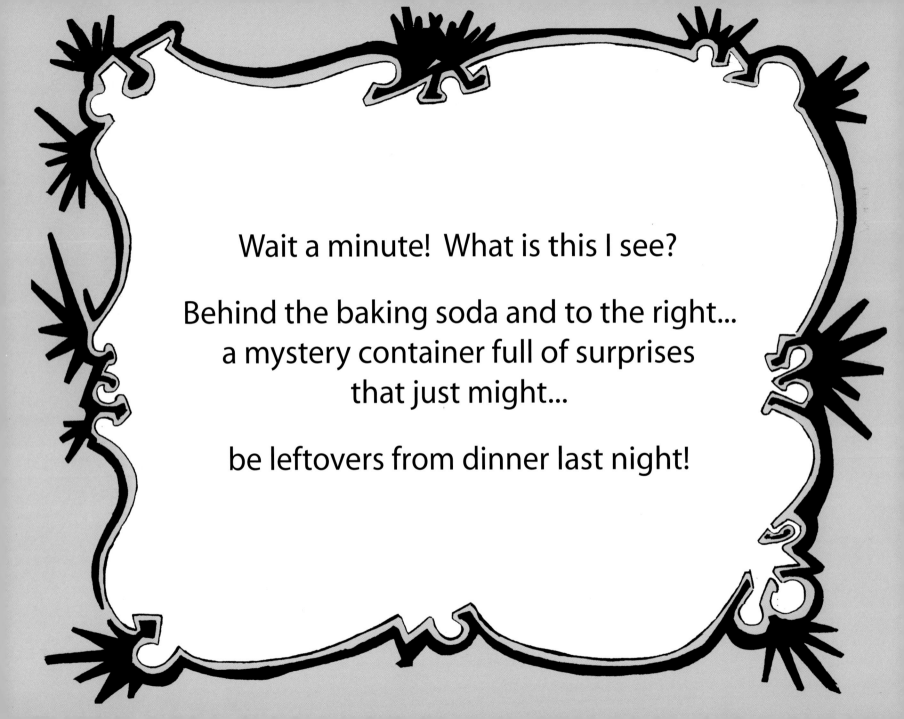

Wait a minute! What is this I see?

Behind the baking soda and to the right...
a mystery container full of surprises
that just might...

be leftovers from dinner last night!

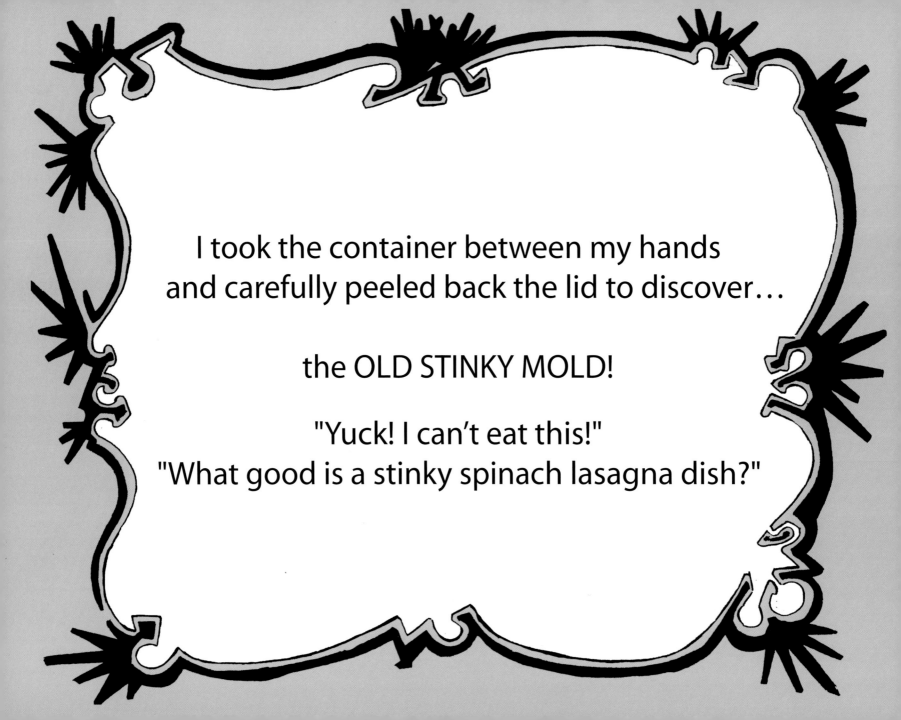

I took the container between my hands
and carefully peeled back the lid to discover…

the OLD STINKY MOLD!

"Yuck! I can't eat this!"
"What good is a stinky spinach lasagna dish?"

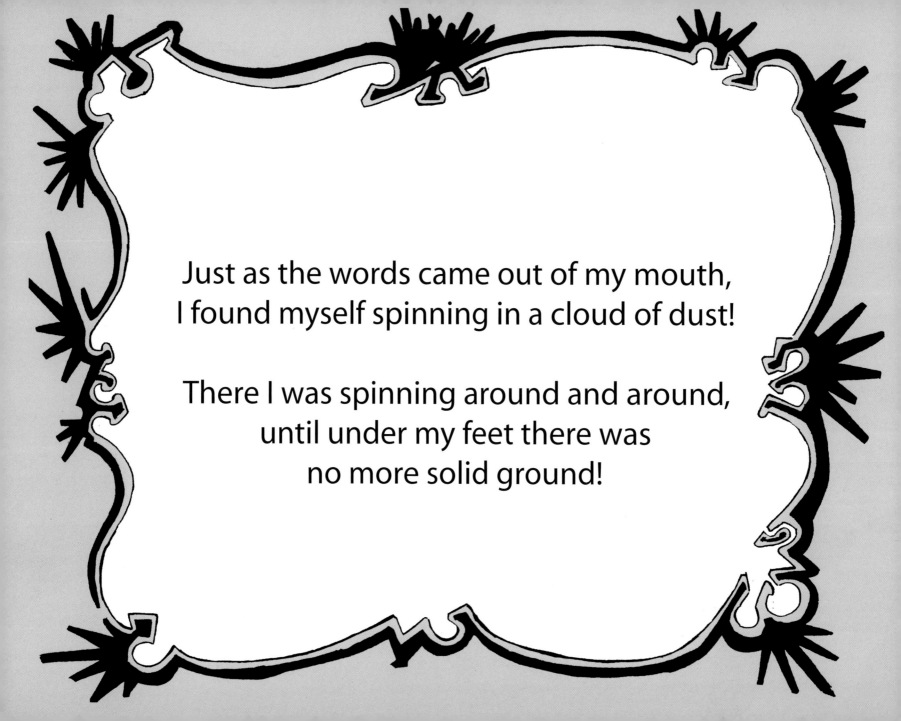

Just as the words came out of my mouth,
I found myself spinning in a cloud of dust!

There I was spinning around and around,
until under my feet there was
no more solid ground!

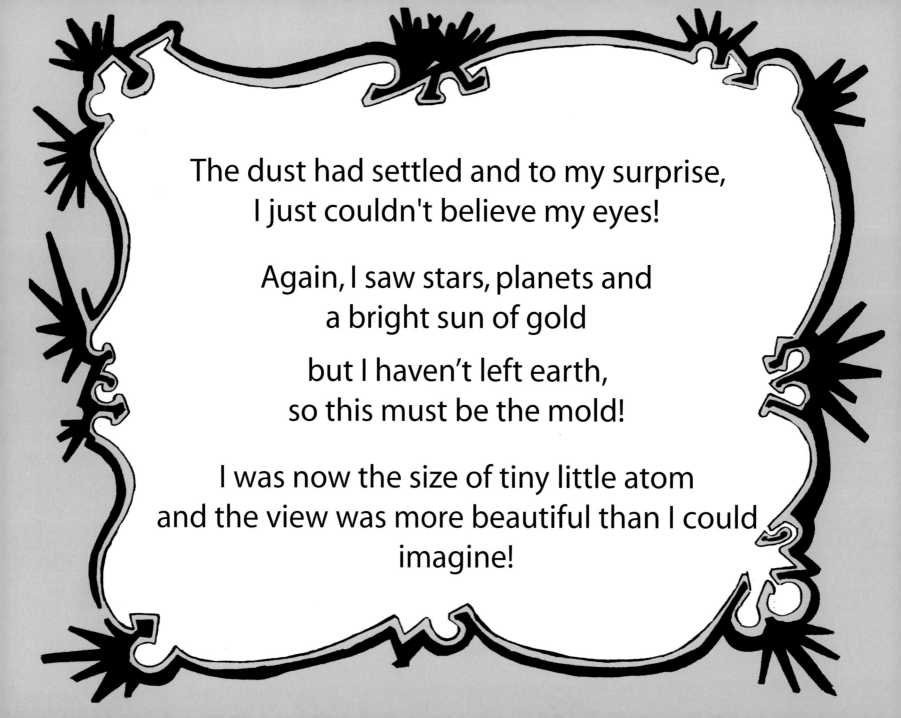

The dust had settled and to my surprise,
I just couldn't believe my eyes!

Again, I saw stars, planets and
a bright sun of gold

but I haven't left earth,
so this must be the mold!

I was now the size of tiny little atom
and the view was more beautiful than I could
imagine!

Chapter Two: Moove

In the distance I saw a planet called Moove.
I was still so hungry and needed some food!

So up and away to Moove I flew.

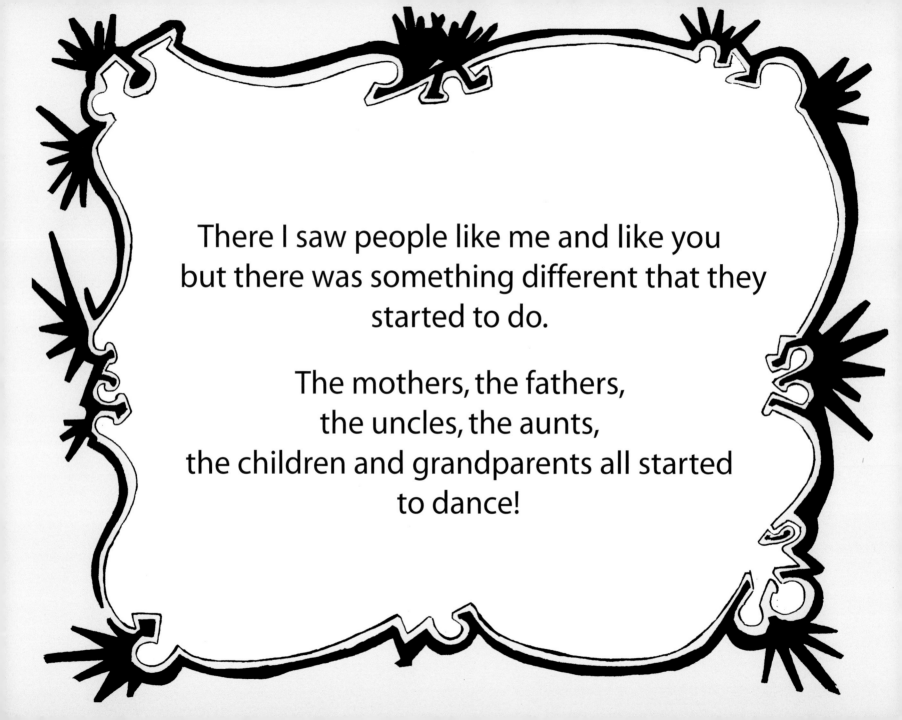

There I saw people like me and like you
but there was something different that they
started to do.

The mothers, the fathers,
the uncles, the aunts,
the children and grandparents all started
to dance!

Two by two they shuffled and twirled.
This must be how they get around in their little
Moove world.

No walking, no running, no cars and
no bikes, just dancing about in
a playful delight.

Instead of running, some chose to Charleston.
The Pogo Hop was a favorite for those
who were jogging.

Ballet was the choice for waiting
and tap dancing worked perfect for parading.

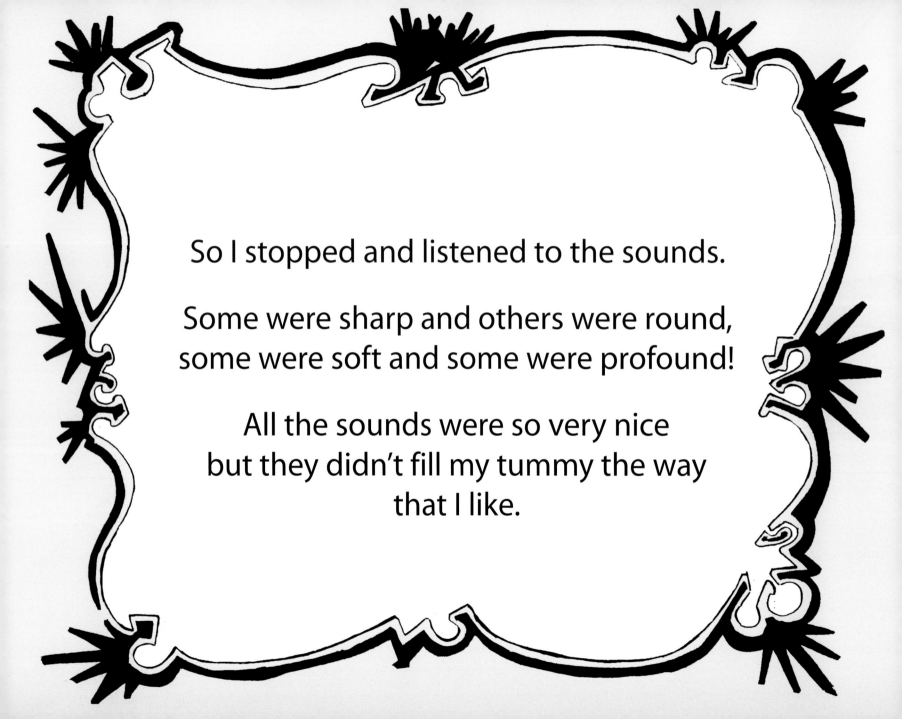

So I stopped and listened to the sounds.

Some were sharp and others were round,
some were soft and some were profound!

All the sounds were so very nice
but they didn't fill my tummy the way
that I like.

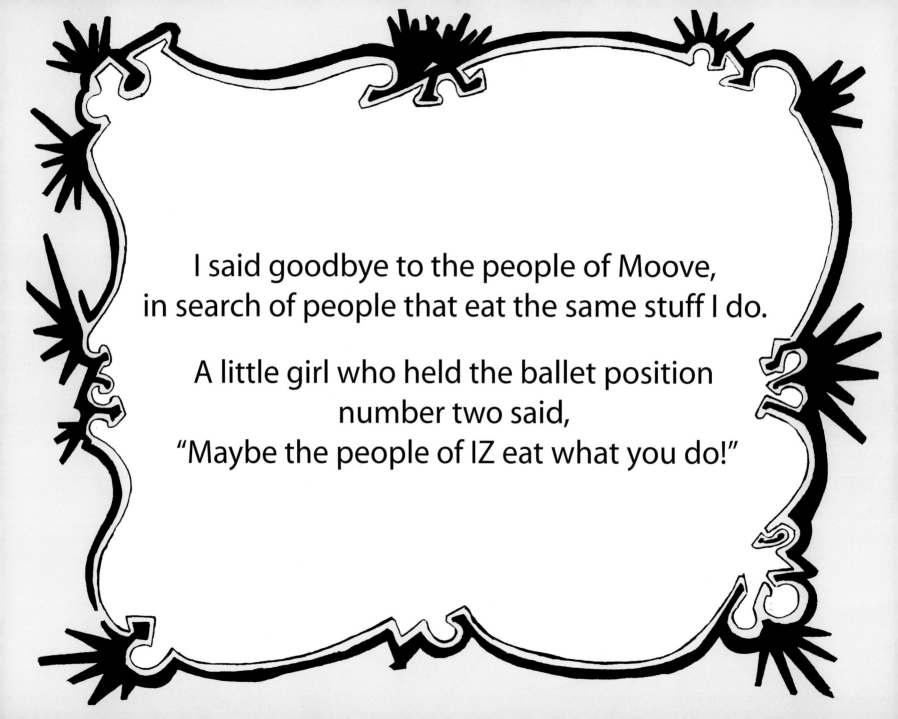

I said goodbye to the people of Moove,
in search of people that eat the same stuff I do.

A little girl who held the ballet position
number two said,
"Maybe the people of IZ eat what you do!"

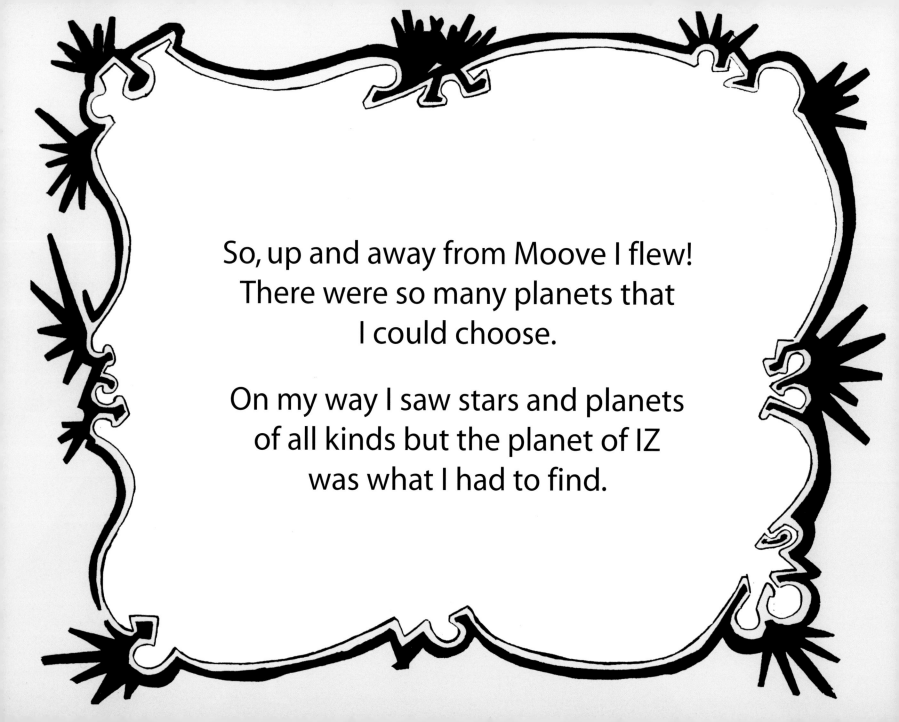

So, up and away from Moove I flew!
There were so many planets that
I could choose.

On my way I saw stars and planets
of all kinds but the planet of IZ
was what I had to find.

Chapter Three: IZ

Far away in the distance of space,
I saw this planet shooting rainbows
all over the place.

It was a beautiful hue of Purple and Blue.
This could be the planet called IZ
that I wanted to go to.

I arrive safely without any surprise
and find the planet of IZ to be so very nice!

No one seems to worry or stress
about the future.
Not one single person regrets the past.

Everyone lives moment by moment
And moments come and go so fast!

The people of IZ are so very pleasant
because the people of IZ live in the present!

People don't push and people don't shove.
People aren't rushing for something
to come.

The people just live in an IZ sort of state.
With the people of IZ, I can relate.

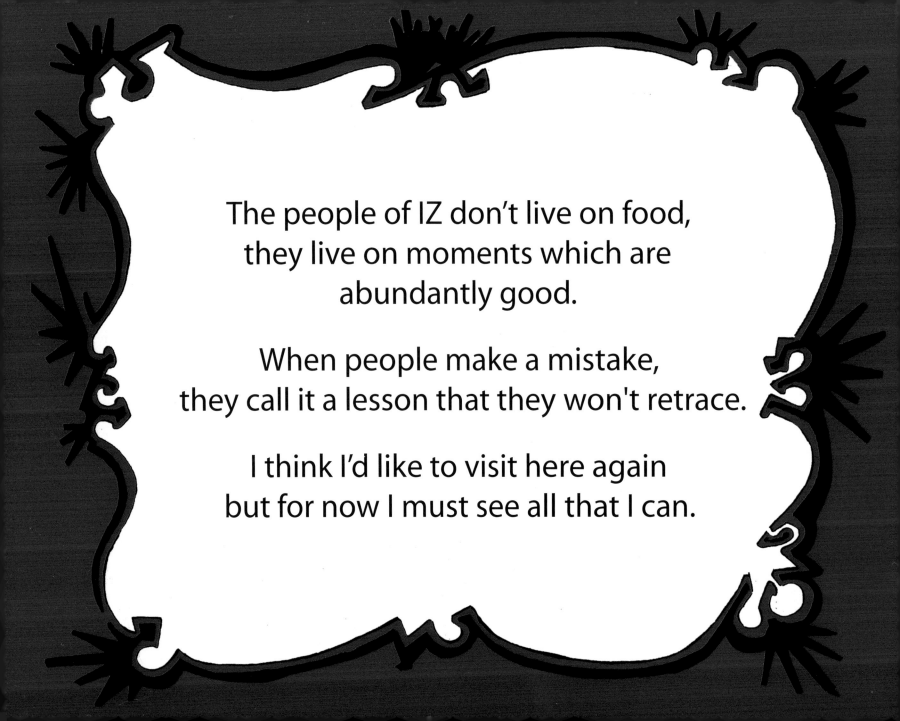

The people of IZ don't live on food,
they live on moments which are
abundantly good.

When people make a mistake,
they call it a lesson that they won't retrace.

I think I'd like to visit here again
but for now I must see all that I can.

So away from the beautiful land of IZ I flew,
still in search of some kind of food.

I'm so very hungry and so very tired,
I just want to go home and have a snooze.

Without a second thought,
I awoke in my bed, to the yummy smell of
pancakes and eggs!

From the kitchen I heard,
"Breakfast is ready!"

Was I still dreaming? Maybe, maybe not…
I know when I ate breakfast,
IT SURE HIT the SPOT!

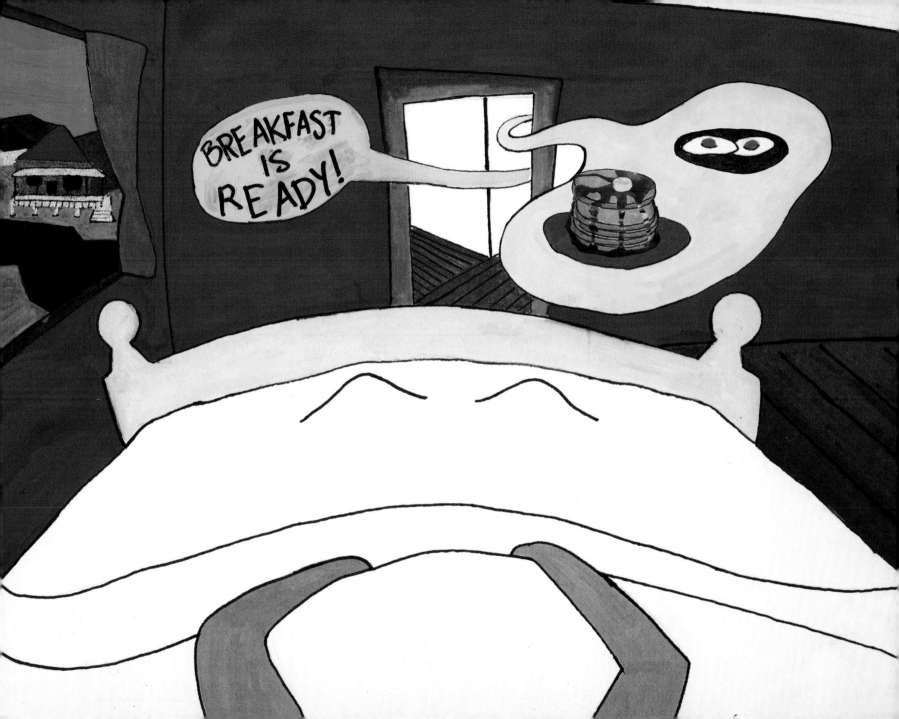

I never looked at things
quite the same way,
whether it was the sky
or breakfast that day.

You might never know what's
beyond the Horizon.
You might never know what's
right under your nose.

Maybe it was a crazy dream
...or maybe it wasn't?

Always LOOK!

Always QUESTION!

Always LISTEN to your HEART!

Always BELIEVE in YOURSELF!

Shanti Wintergate and Gregory Attonito

www.shantimusic.com - www.myspace.com/gregattonito - www.hollywoodjersey.com

Shanti Wintergate and Gregory Attonito never planned to become a children's book author/illustrator team but this power couple seem to do it all. Playfully calling themselves "Super Buddies," they dive into anything and everything creative. It all started one day while Shanti was sipping tea and having a snack at The Rose Cafe in Venice, CA. "I was sitting there when this little poem just had to come out!" So, on a napkin she wrote the first ten lines of what was to become, I Went for a Walk. What started out as ten little lines grew into an amazing story that captures the imagination and sends it flying into the stratosphere. The conception of the story happened in a few days but finding just the right illustrator was a longer journey that led to a marriage and a few trips around the world.

Shanti has been an artist all her life. Born in Hollywood, CA to an artistic and musical family from Victoria, BC, she evolved into a real Renaissance Woman as she grew up. Bursting with a passion for science and an imagination that is clearly endless, Shanti is always writing that next album, acting in that next film or TV show, painting, designing, taking photographs or exploring something new. She continues to have success in her music with radio play across the US and South America and placements of her songs can be heard on the WB's Charmed, Joan of Arcadia and MTV's Laguna Beach. Items of Shanti's can be seen on display at the Rock and Roll Hall of Fame's "Warped: 12 Years of Music, Mayhem and More" exhibit. Most recently she has snagged a guest starring role as "Hallie on Wheels," a roller derby girl suspected of murder on the top rated TV show CSI: NY.

Gregory Attonito has been the singer of the legendary New Jersey punk band The Bouncing Souls for the better part of the last 20 years. He has toured around the world more times than he can remember with the likes of My Chemical Romance, Green Day, Against Me!, NOFX, Bad Religion, The Ramones, Blondie, Max Weinberg, and countless others. This Jersey boy could take you on a tour of almost any public transit system worldwide with ease. With seven full length albums under his belt, more frequent flyer miles than he can count and his worn-out shirt and tie stating "So Rad" on display at the Rock and Roll Hall of Fame, Gregory is an icon when it comes to D.I.Y. In recent years, the constant touring of The Bouncing Souls left little time for other projects but times are-a-changin' and this creative genius has begun showing us that there's more to him than just an amazing front man. His MySpace page sings a different tune, displaying his artwork and self-produced and recorded music. In addition to singing, Greg loves to paint, play guitar, piano, bass, drums and a little ukulele!

Super powers Shanti and Gregory found each other in 1997 in a little village in India. Yes, India...but that story is far too long so we'll fast forward some. They fell in love, they got married, and that brings us back to The Rose Cafe and the first few lines of their newest creation together, I Went for a Walk.

I Went for a Walk was created all over the world. From the illustrations to the story, pieces of this book were inspired, written and drawn while traveling and exploring our amazing planet. Throughout an international tour with his band, The Bouncing Souls, Gregory carried along the story that Shanti wrote with his sketchbook and a bag full of paint pens. He hiked up mountain trails in Italy and Switzerland, explored the bustle of downtown Tokyo, gazed at the waves in Australia from a rocky cliff and sometimes just sat on a park bench enjoying the everyday comings and goings of a small village. All the while, he infused the moment into whatever drawing he was creating, hoping that some part of all these moments would be felt by the reader.

We hope this story creates a time and a place for you to sit down and appreciate the expansive universe within and all around us. Time flies by before you know it, so celebrate your family, your life and yourself now. You are beautiful. Remember: You are the manifestation of your imagination and we love you!

Love,
Shanti and Gregory

photos by: Justin Harris

"Making something from nothing since 1997"
Hollywood Jersey
164 Silver Fox Trail
McCall, ID 83638
info@hollywoodjersey.com
www.hollywoodjersey.com

Text and Illustrations © 2007 Shanti Wintergate and Gregory Attonito
This edition published in 2007

ISBN 978-0-9795426-0-2

For ordering information please visit us at:
www.iwentforawalk.com

Special thanks to our loving families and friends, en particular un profundo agradecimiento a nuestra hermosa
familia de amor en Guatemala.